JOSEPH MIDTHUN   SAMUEL HITI

BUILDING BLOCKS OF MATHEMATICS

MULTIPLICATION

WORLD
BOOK

a Scott Fetzer company
Chicago

www.worldbook.com

World Book, Inc.
233 N. Michigan Avenue
Chicago, IL 60601
U.S.A.

For information about other World Book publications,
visit our website at www.worldbook.com
or call 1-800-WORLDBK (967-5325).
For information about sales to schools and libraries,
call 1-800-975-3250 (United States),
or 1-800-837-5365 (Canada).

Library of Congress Cataloging-in-Publication Data

Multiplication.

    pages cm. -- (Building blocks of mathematics)
   Summary: "A graphic nonfiction volume that
introduces critical multiplication concepts"-- Provided
by publisher.
   Includes index.
   ISBN 978-0-7166-1435-7 -- ISBN 978-0-7166-1476-0
(pbk.)
   1. Multiplication--Comic books, strips, etc.--Juvenile
literature. 2. Graphic novels. I. World Book, Inc.
QA115.M83 2013
513.2'13--dc23

                        2012031036

Building Blocks of Mathematics
ISBN: 978-0-7166-1431-9 (set, hc.)

Printed in China by Shenzhen Donnelley
Printing Co., Ltd., Guangdong Province
2nd printing October 2013

Acknowledgments:
Created by Samuel Hiti and Joseph Midthun
Art by Samuel Hiti
Written by Joseph Midthun
Special thanks to Anita Wager, Hala
Ghousseini, and Syril McNally.

STAFF
Executive Committee
President: Donald D. Keller
Vice President and Editor in Chief:
   Paul A. Kobasa
Vice President, Sales & Marketing:
   Sean Lockwood
Vice President, International: Richard Flower
Director, Human Resources: Bev Ecker

Editorial
Manager, Series and Trade: Cassie Mayer
Writer and Letterer: Joseph Midthun
Manager, Contracts & Compliance
   (Rights & Permissions): Loranne K. Shields

Manufacturing/Pre-Press
Director: Carma Fazio
Manufacturing Manager: Steven Hueppchen
Production/Technology Manager:
   Anne Fritzinger
Proofreader: Emilie Schrage

Graphics and Design
Senior Manager, Graphics and Design: Tom Evans
Coordinator, Design Development and
   Production: Brenda B. Tropinski
Book Design: Samuel Hiti

TABLE OF CONTENTS

Our drawings are coming to life...

Monsters!

...and they're growing!

PLOP PLOP PLOP PLOP

Do you notice what they all have in common?

Each one has 4 legs!

So, let's figure out how many legs they have all together!

Hey!

I'm seeing double!

Double 4 and double 4!

10

When you multiply two numbers, you are adding up equal groups.

For instance, here's a group of 6 flowers!

PLOP   PLOP

And there are 5 bees on each flower.

Bees?!

Don't take my word for it, have a look!

12

See?

That's 6 groups of 5.

So, how many bees are there all together?

Let's skip count by 5!

Okay!

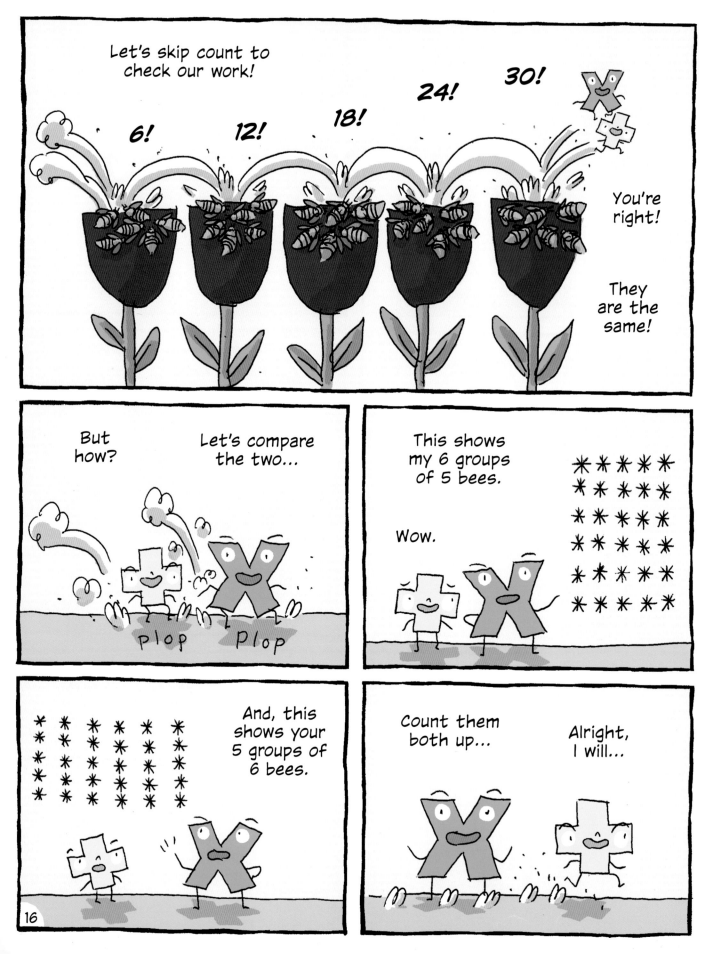

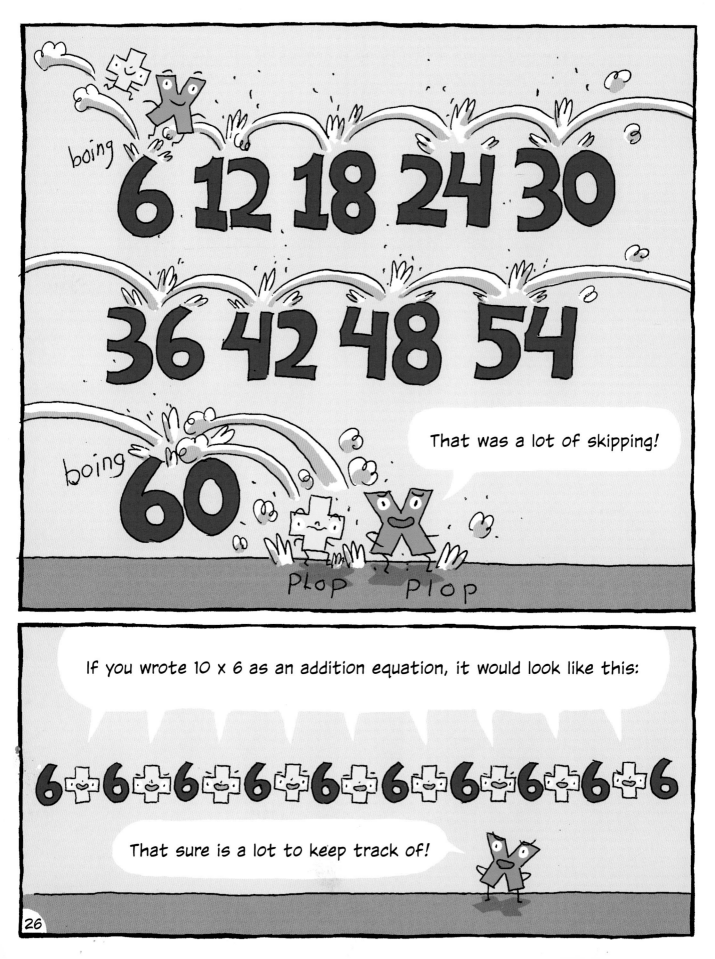

6 12 18 24 30

36 42 48 54

boing 60

That was a lot of skipping!

If you wrote 10 x 6 as an addition equation, it would look like this:

6 + 6 + 6 + 6 + 6 + 6 + 6 + 6 + 6 + 6

That sure is a lot to keep track of!

MULTIPLICATION FACTS

This table can help you multiply as easy as 1, 2, 3!
It can also help you learn your multiplication facts.

HERE'S HOW IT WORKS:

1. Choose a number from the column on the left.
2. Then choose a number from the top row of the table.
3. Find the point where the two numbers meet.

YOU'VE FOUND THE PRODUCT OF THE TWO NUMBERS!

X	0	1	2	3	4	5	6	7	8	9	10
0	0	0	0	0	0	0	0	0	0	0	0
1	0	1	2	3	4	5	6	7	8	9	10
2	0	2	4	6	8	10	12	14	16	18	20
3	0	3	6	9	12	15	18	21	24	27	30
4	0	4	8	12	16	20	24	28	32	36	40
5	0	5	10	15	20	25	30	35	40	45	50
6	0	6	12	18	24	30	36	42	48	54	60
7	0	7	14	21	28	35	42	49	56	63	70
8	0	8	16	24	32	40	48	56	64	72	80
9	0	9	18	27	36	45	54	63	72	81	90
10	0	10	20	30	40	50	60	70	80	90	100

FOR EXAMPLE:

1 x 0 = 0; 1 x 2 = 2; 1 x 3 = 3; and so on!

FIND OUT MORE

BOOKS

7 x 9 = Trouble!
    by Claudia Mills and G. Brian Karas
    (Farrar Straus Giroux, 2002)

The Best of Times: Math
Strategies that Multiply
    by Greg Tang and Harry Briggs
    (Scholastic Press, 2002)

Breakfast at Danny's Diner
    by Judith Bauer Stamper
    and Chris L. Demarest
    (Grosset and Dunlap, 2003)

Double the Ducks
    by Stuart J. Murphy and
    Valeria Petrone (HarperCollins
    Publishers, 2003)

Eggs and Legs: Counting by Twos
    by Michael Dahl and Todd Ouren
    (Picture Window Books, 2005)

If You Were a Times Sign
    by Trisha Speed Shaskan
    and Sarah Dillard (Picture
    Window Books, 2009)

Mathemania
    by Raymond Blum and Jeff Sinclair
    (Sterling Publishing Co., 2001)

Multiply on the Fly
    by Suzanne Slade and Erin E. Hunter
    (Sylvan Dell Publishers, 2011)

Multiply This!
    by Melanie Chrismer and Ari Ginsburg
    (Children's Press, 2005)

Sixteen Runaway Pumpkins
    by Dianne Ochiltree and
    Anne-Sophie Lanquetin
    (M.K. McElderry Books, 2004)

WEBSITES

Cool Math 4 Kids: Times Tables
    www.coolmath4kids.com/times-tables
    Lessons, practice activities, and
    flashcards make this website
    a useful resource for kids interested
    in improving their multiplication skills.

Fun 4 the Brain: Multiplication
    www.fun4thebrain.com/mult.html
    At this educational website, games
    and printable worksheets teach
    essential multiplication strategies.

Kids' Numbers
    www.kidsnumbers.com/
    multiplication.php
    Prepare with week-by-week
    multiplication practice lessons
    and games.

Multiplication.com
    www.multiplication.com/games
    There are lots of ways to use
    multiplication. Try out a few with
    the games on this website!

Play Kids' Games: Math Games
    www.playkidsgames.com/
    mathgames.htm
    Test your math knowledge with
    fun games and quizzes.

NOTE TO EDUCATORS

This volume supports a conceptual understanding of multiplication through a series of story problems. As the Multiplication and Addition characters solve each story problem, they present different strategies, including variations of direct modeling, counting, and invented strategies. Below is an index of strategies that appear in this volume. For more information about how to use these strategies in the classroom, see the list of Educator Resources at the bottom of this page.

Index of Strategies

Educator Resources

Children's Mathematics: Cognitively Guided Instruction
    by Thomas Carpenter, Elizabeth Fennema, Megan L. Franke, Linda Levi, and Susan B. Empson (Heinemann, 1999)

Elementary and Middle School Mathematics: Teaching Developmentally
    by John A. Van de Walle, Karen S. Karp, and Jennifer M. Bay-Williams (Harcourt, 2013)

Knowing and Teaching Elementary Mathematics: Teachers' Understanding of Fundamental Mathematics in China and the United States
    by Liping Ma (Routledge, 2010)

Young Mathematicians at Work:
Constructing Multiplication and Division
    by Catherine Twomey Fosnot and Maarten Dolk (Heinemann, 2011)